To Maya, a true tortilla fan, and to friends old and new, who love large, round, floppy, flappy, slightly singed, just-off-the-stovetop tortillas —R. G. T.

To my aunts Irma, Amelia, Adela, Gloria, Julia, Yolanda, and Grace, for all those wonderful winter tamales and summer barbeque memories —J. P.

Library of Congress Cataloging-in-Publication Data available
ISBN 978-1-4521-0616-8

Book design by Eloise Leigh.
Typeset in Brandon Grotesque.
The illustrations in this book were rendered in paint.

Manufactured in China.

3 5 7 9 10 8 6 4 2

Chronicle Books LLC
680 Second Street, San Francisco, California 94107

www.chroniclekids.com

ROUND
Is a
TORTILLA

A Book of Shapes

By Roseanne Greenfield Thong
Illustrated by John Parra

chronicle books·san francisco

Round are *sombreros*.
Round is the moon.
Round are the trumpets
that blare out a tune.

Round are *campanas*
that chime and ring.

Round are the nests
where swallows sing.

Round are *tortillas* and *tacos*, too.
Round is a pot of *abuela's* stew.
I can name more round things. Can you?

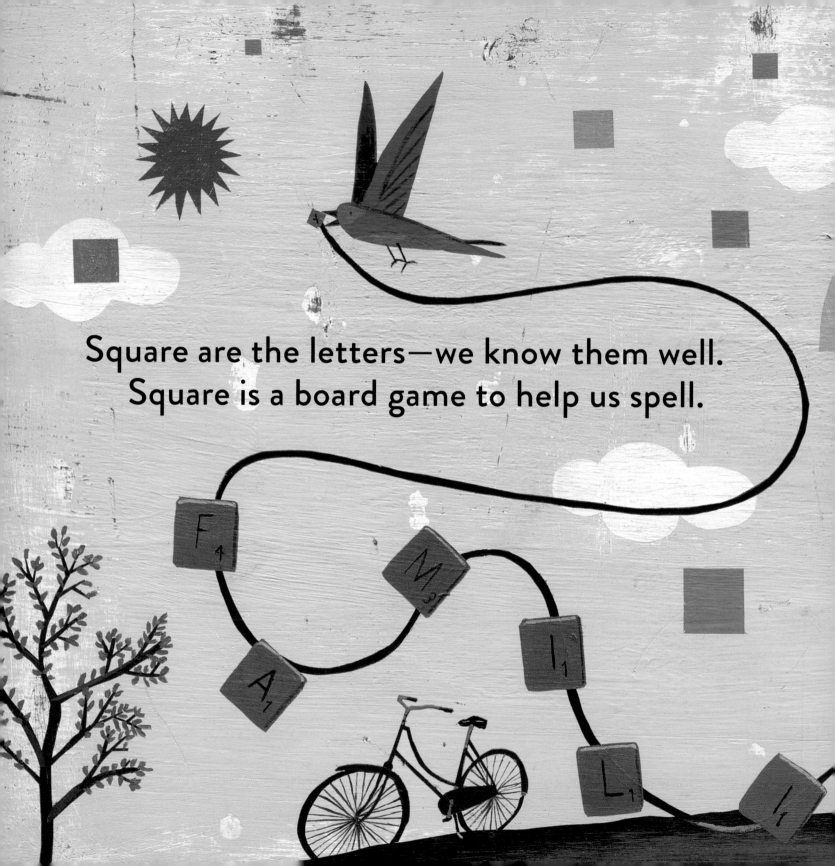

Square are the letters—we know them well.
Square is a board game to help us spell.

Square are *ventanas*
that give a view.
Square is my clock,
and my photos, too.

Square is the park, and the *zócalo*.
Square is a fountain from long ago.
How many square things do you know?

Rectangles are carts
with bells that chime
and cold *paletas*
in summertime.

Stone *metates* inside our *casa*
help us grind our corn to *masa*.

Rectangles are flags that fly
above the scoreboard, way up high.
How many rectangles do you spy?

Triangles are crunchy chips
for *guacamole* and other dips.

Triangles sail on the breeze.
They line the shore and glide on seas.

Sandías chilled in tubs of ice,
   quesadillas by the slice—
triangles can beat the heat.
   What other triangles can you eat?

Oval is my favorite locket,
a special pebble in my pocket.

I find ovals at the store,
huevos, olives, beans galore.
Can you name a couple more?

Stars for parties, stars for light,
lining streets with colors bright.
There are so many shapes wherever you go.
How many more shapes do you know?

GLOSSARY

ABUELA: Grandmother.

ABUELA'S STEW (POZOLE): Grandmothers love to make a special stew called *pozole* on the weekends. *Pozole* is made with *hominy* (large kernels of corn soaked in lime water and dried), and often contains pork, chili, seasonings, and vegetables.

ATÚN: Tuna.

CAMPANAS: Bells. Large *campanas* hang in church towers throughout South and Central America, and chime before celebrations and church services to let worshippers know that it's time to start.

CASA: House.

CUADRADO: Square.

FAMILIA: Family.

GUACAMOLE: A mixture of mashed avocado, chopped onion, tomato, chili pepper, and seasoning, served as a dip for chips or in salads.

HUEVOS: Eggs.

MARIACHIS: Musicians who stroll through the streets (or nowadays play in restaurants), dressed in fine suits with wide-brimmed hats, and who sing ballads accompanied by guitars, trumpets, and violins.

MASA: Corn flour, eaten daily and used for Mexican foods like *tamales* (packets of filled, steamed dough) and *tortillas*.

METATE: A flat or slightly hollowed piece of rock, used with a stone rolling pin called a *mano*. Between the rock and the rolling pin, grain is crushed into meal.

PALETAS: Mexican-style ice-cream or frozen-fruit bars on sticks. Traditional fruit-bar flavors include mango, guava, tamarind and pineapple, and ice-cream flavors include vanilla, chocolate, strawberry, and coconut.

PLAZAS: Public squares or marketplaces.

QUESADILLA: A *tortilla* folded over a filling of hot, melted cheese.

SANDÍA: Watermelon.

SOMBRERO: A Mexican hat made of straw or felt, with a pointed top and an extra-wide brim to shade the head, neck, and shoulders. The name comes from the Spanish word *sombra*, which means "shade."

SUEÑOS: Dreams.

TACO: A *tortilla*, sometimes folded, sometimes flat, piled with fillings like ground meat, cheese, and lettuce, and served hot.

TORTILLAS: Large, round, flatbread pancakes, made from *masa* (corn flour dough) or wheat, and baked on a hot surface. (In Spain, *tortillas* are thick egg omelets fried with potatoes.)

VENTANAS: Windows.

ZÓCALO: Every town and city in Mexico has a *zócalo* or main square, often filled with shady trees, gardens, benches, and fountains. People young and old gather to chat, rest, look at artwork, and listen to bands and entertainers.